# A
# CHRISTMAS
## TREASURY

Michael O'Mara Books Limited

First published in Great Britain in 2000 by
Michael O'Mara Books Limited
9 Lion Yard, Tremadoc Road
London SW4 7NQ

The publisher would like to thank Brenda and Gareth Davies for their help in researching illustrative material.

A CIP catalogue record for this book is available from the British Library

ISBN 1-85479-588-0

1 3 5 7 9 10 8 6 4 2

Designed by Mick Keates
Typeset by Concise Artisans

Printed and bound in Singapore by Tien Wah Press

# CONTENTS

# Gabriel's Message

Basque carol

The angel Gabriel from Heaven came,
His wings as drifted snow, his eyes as flame;
'All hail,' said he, 'thou lowly maiden, Mary,
Most highly favoured lady,' *Gloria!*

'For known a blessed mother thou shalt be,
All generations laud and honour thee,
Thy Son shall be Emmanuel, by seers foretold,
Most highly favoured lady,' *Gloria!*

Then gently Mary meekly bowed her head,
'To me be as it pleaseth God,' she said,
'My soul shall laud and magnify His holy name.'
Most highly favoured lady, *Gloria!*

Of her, Emmanuel, the Christ, was born
In Bethlehem, all on a Christmas morn,
And Christian folk throughout the world will ever say:
Most highly favoured lady, *Gloria!*

Words by Rev S. Baring-Gould

Heap on more wood! — the wind is chill,
But let it whistle as it will,
We'll keep our Christmas merry still.

Sir Walter Scott

A good conscience is a continual Christmas.

Benjamin Franklin

Christmas! 'Tis the season for kindling
the fire of hospitality in the hall, the genial fire
of charity in the heart.

Washington Irving

I will honour Christmas in my heart and try
to keep it all the year.

Charles Dickens

# OLD CHRISTMAS

WASHINGTON IRVING

Here were kept up the old games of hoodman blind, shoe the wild mare, hot cockles, steal the white loaf, bob apple, and snapdragon: the Yule-log and Christmas candle were regularly burnt, and the mistletoe, with its white berries, hung up to the imminent peril of the housemaids.

# DULCE DOMUM

'I think it must be the field-mice,' replied the Mole, with a touch of pride in his manner...

'Let's have a look at them!' cried the Rat, jumping up and running to the door.

It was a pretty sight, and a seasonable one, that met their eyes when they flung the door open. In the fore-court, lit by the dim rays of a horn lantern, some eight or ten little field-mice stood in a semi-circle, red worsted comforters round their throats, their fore-paws thrust deep into their pockets, their feet jigging for warmth. With bright beady eyes they glanced shyly at each other, sniggering a little, sniffing and applying coat-sleeves a good deal. As the door opened, one of the elder ones that carried the lantern was just saying, 'Now then, one, two, three!' and forthwith their shrill little voices uprose on the air, singing one of the old-time carols that their forefathers composed in fields that were fallow and held by frost, or when snow-bound in chimney corners, and handed down to be sung in the miry streets to lamp-lit windows at Yule-time.

CAROL

Villagers all, this frosty tide,
Let your doors swing open wide,
Though wind may follow, and snow beside,
Yet draw us in by your fire to bide;
Joy shall be yours in the morning!

Here we stand in the cold and the sleet,
Blowing fingers and stamping feet,
Come from far away you to greet —
You by the fire and we in the street —
Bidding you joy in the morning!

For ere one half of the night was gone,
Sudden a star has led us on,
Raining bliss and benison —
Bliss to-morrow and more anon,
Joy for every morning!

Goodman Joseph toiled through the snow —
Saw the star o'er a stable low;
Mary she might not further go —
Welcome thatch, and litter below!
Joy was hers in the morning!

And then they heard the angels tell
'Who were the first to cry Nowell?
Animals all, as it befell,
In the stable where they did dwell!
Joy shall be theirs in the morning!'

KENNETH GRAHAME, *The Wind in the Willows*

9

# THE GLASTONBURY THORN

The legend of the Glastonbury thorn has its origins in Christ's death as well as in the celebration of his birth. The legend goes that soon after the death of Christ, Joseph of Arimathea travelled from the Holy Land to Britain to spread the message of Christianity. Tired out from his journey, he lay down to rest, pushing his staff into the ground beside him. When he awoke, he found that the staff had taken root and had begun to grow and blossom. It is said he left it there and it has flowered every Christmas and every spring. Legend has it that a Puritan who was trying to cut down the tree was prevented from doing so by being blinded by a splinter of the wood as he hacked at it. The original thorn did eventually die but not before many cuttings had been taken. It is one of these very cuttings, they say, which is in the grounds of Glastonbury Abbey today.

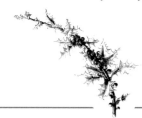

# No Chamber in the Inn

Anonymous

Yet if his majesty our sovereign lord
Should of his own accord
Friendly himself invite,
And say 'I'll be your guest tomorrow night,'
How should we stir ourselves, call and
    command
All hand to work! 'Let no man idle stand.
Set me fine Spanish tables in the hall,
See they be fitted all;
Let there be room to eat,
And order taken that there want no meat.
See every sconce and candlestick made bright
That without tapers they may give a light.
Look to the presence: are the carpets spread,
The dais o'er the head,
The cushions in the chairs,
And all the candles lighted on the stairs?
Perfume the chambers, and in any case
Let each man give attendance in his place.'
Thus if the king were coming would we do,
And 'twere good reason too;

For 'tis a duteous thing
To show all honour to an earthly king,
And after all our travail and our cost,
So he be pleased, to think no labour cost.
But at the coming of the King of Heaven
All's set at six and seven:
We wallow in our sin,
Christ cannot find a chamber in the inn.
We entertain him always like a stranger,
And as at first still lodge him in the manger.

# Christmas-tree Land

Mrs Molesworth

And there it was – the most beautiful they had yet seen – all radiant with light and glistening with every pretty present child-heart could desire.

'We are only to look at it, you know,' said Maia; 'it has to be packed up and sent us, like the others. But,' she stopped short, 'who is that, Rollo,' she went on, 'standing just by the tree? Can it be Santa Claus himself come to see if it is all right?'

'Santa Claus,' exclaimed a well-known voice, 'Santa Claus, indeed! Is that your new name for me, my Maia?'

Then came a cry of joy – a cry from two little loving hearts – a cry which rang merry echoes through the forest, and at which, though it woke up lots of little birds snugly hidden away in the warmest corners they could find, no one thought of grumbling, except, I think, an old owl, who greatly objected to any disturbance of his nightly promenades and meditations.

'Papa, papa, dear papa!' was the cry. 'Papa, you have come back to us. That was what godmother meant,' they said together. And their father, well pleased, held them in his arms as if he would never let them go.

# O CHRISTMAS TREE

O Christmas tree, O Christmas tree!
How are thy leaves so verdant!
O Christmas tree, O Christmas tree,
How are thy leaves so verdant!
Not only in the summertime,
But even in winter is thy prime.
O Christmas tree, O Christmas tree,
How are thy leaves so verdant!
O Christmas tree, O Christmas tree,
Much pleasure doth thou bring me!
O Christmas tree, O Christmas tree,
Much pleasure doth thou bring me!
For every year the Christmas tree,
Brings to us all both joy and glee.
O Christmas tree, O Christmas tree,
Much pleasure doth thou bring me!
O Christmas tree, O Christmas tree,
Thy candles shine out brightly!
O Christmas tree, O Christmas tree,
Thy candles shine out brightly!
Each bough doth hold its tiny light,
That makes each toy to sparkle bright.
O Christmas tree, O Christmas tree,
Thy candles shine out brightly!

# The Birth of Christ

as told by SAINT LUKE

And she brought forth her first-born son, and wrapped him in swaddling clothes, and laid him in a manger; because there was no room for them in the inn.

And there were in the same country shepherds abiding in the field, keeping watch over their flock by night.

And, lo, the angel of the Lord came upon them, and the glory of the Lord shone around about them; and they were sore afraid.

And the angel said unto them, Fear not: for, behold, I bring you good tidings of great joy, which shall be to all people.

For unto to you is born this day in the city of David a Saviour, which is Christ the Lord.

And this shall be a sign unto you; ye shall find the babe wrapped in swaddling clothes, lying in a manger.

And suddenly there was with the angel a multitude of the heavenly host praising God, and saying,

Glory to God in the highest, and on earth peace, good will toward men.

LUKE 2: 7-14

# JOY TO THE WORLD

Joy to the world! The Lord is come:
Let earth receive her King.
Let ev'ry heart prepare Him room,
And heaven and nature sing,
And heaven and nature sing,
And heaven and heaven and nature sing.

He rules the world with truth and grace,
And makes the nations prove
The glories of His righteousness
And wonders of His love,
And wonders of His love,
And wonders, wonders of His love.

# A Christmas Carol

CHARLES DICKENS

'A merry Christmas, Uncle! God save you!' cried a cheerful voice. It was the voice of Scrooge's nephew, who came upon him so quickly that this was the first intimation he had of his approach.

'Bah!' said Scrooge. 'Humbug!'

He had so heated himself with rapid walking in the fog and frost, this nephew of Scrooge's, that he was all in a glow; his face was ruddy and handsome; his eyes sparkled, and his breath smoked again.

'Christmas a humbug, Uncle!' said Scrooge's nephew. 'You don't mean that, I am sure?'

'I do,' said Scrooge. 'Merry Christmas! What right have you to be merry? What reason have you to be merry? You're poor enough.'

'Come, then,' returned the nephew gaily. 'What right have you to be dismal? What reason have you to be morose? You're rich enough.'

Scrooge having no better answer ready on the spur of the moment, said, 'Bah!' again; and followed it up with 'Humbug'.

# OLD CHRISTMAS

WASHINGTON IRVING

Now Christmas is come,
Let us beat up the drum,
And call all our neighbours together;
And when they appear,
Let us make them such cheer
As will keep out the wind and the weather.

# ADVENT WREATHS

The origins of the Advent wreath are found in the folk practices of the pre-Christian Germanic peoples who, during the cold December darkness of Eastern Europe, gathered wreaths of evergreen and lighted fires as signs of hope in a coming spring and renewed light. Christians kept these popular traditions alive, and by the sixteenth century Catholics and Protestants throughout Germany used these symbols to celebrate their Advent hope in Christ, the everlasting Light. From Germany the use of the Advent wreath spread to other parts of the Christian world.

# O Come, O Come, Emmanuel

translation by T. A. Lacey

O come, O come, Emmanuel!
Redeem thy captive Israel,
That into exile drear has gone,
Far from the face of God's dear Son.
*Rejoice! Rejoice! Emmanuel*
*Shall come to thee, O Israel.*

O come, thou branch of Jesse! Draw
The quarry from the lion's claw:
From the dread caverns of the grave,
From nether hell, thy people save .
*Rejoice!* . . .

O come, O come, thou Dayspring bright!
Pour on our souls thy healing light;
Dispel the long night's lingering gloom,
And pierce the shadows of the tomb.
*Rejoice!* . . .

O come, thou Lord of David's Key,
The royal door fling wide and free;
Safeguard for us the heavenward road,
And bar the way to death's abode.
*Rejoice!* . . .

O come, O come, Adonaï!
Who in thy glorious majesty
From that high mountain, clothed in awe,
Gavest thy folk the elder Law.
*Rejoice!* . . .

# A PRAYER

MARTIN LUTHER

Ah, dearest Jesus, holy Child,
Make thee a bed, soft, undefiled,
Within my heart, that it may be
A quiet chamber kept for Thee.
My heart for very joy doth leap,
My lips no more can silence keep,
I too must sing, with joyful tongue,
That sweetest ancient cradle song,
Glory to God in highest heaven,
Who unto man His Son hath given
While angels sing with pious mirth.
A glad new year to all the earth.

# INFANT HOLY

Infant holy, infant lowly
For His bed a cattle stall
Oxen lowing, little knowing
Christ the Babe is Lord of all
Swift are winging, angels singing
Nowells ringing, tidings bringing
Christ the Babe is Lord of all
Flocks were sleeping, shepherds keeping
Vigil till the morning new
Saw the glory, heard the story
Tidings of a gospel true
Thus rejoicing, free from sorrow
Praises voicing, greet the new
Christ the Babe was born for you.

# A CHRISTMAS TREE

CHARLES DICKENS

I have been looking on, this evening, at a merry company of children assembled round that pretty German toy, a Christmas Tree. The tree was planted in the middle of a great round table, and towered high above their heads. It was brilliantly lighted by a multitude of little tapers; and everywhere sparkled and glittered with bright objects.

# CHRISTMAS TREE LEGENDS

It seems to be generally recognized that the people who lived in what is now Germany were the first to develop the tradition of the Christmas tree. Many legends exist about its origins. One is the story of Saint Boniface, an English monk who organized the Christian Church in France and Germany. One day, travelling through Germany, he came upon a group of pagans gathered around a great oak tree about to sacrifice a child to their god. In anger, and to stop the sacrifice and save the child's life, Boniface felled the tree with one mighty blow of his fist. In its place grew a small fir tree. The saint told the pagan worshippers that the tiny fir was the Tree of Life and stood for the eternal life of Christ.

Another legend tells of a poor woodsman who long ago met a lost and hungry child on Christmas Eve. Though very poor himself, the woodsman gave the child food and shelter for the night. The next morning the man awoke to find a beautiful glittering tree outside his door. The hungry child, it was said, was really the Christ Child in disguise. He created the tree to reward the good man for his charity.

Others feel the origin of the Christmas tree may lie in the medieval Paradise Play. Most people in those days could not read and, all over Europe, plays were used to teach the lessons of the Bible. The Paradise Play, which showed the creation of man and the fall of Adam and Eve from the Garden of Eden was performed every year on 24 December. As it was winter, there was a slight problem: an apple tree was needed, but apple trees do not bear fruit – or leaves – in winter so an evergreen was hung about with apples and used instead. Nowadays, the baubles hung on Christmas trees often include shiny red apples.

Martin Luther is credited with first placing candles on the Christmas tree. After his banishment from the Catholic church he spent a great deal of time walking through the forests of evergreen conifers thinking through his beliefs. He was awed by the beauty of millions of stars glimmering through the trees, and was so taken by the sight that he cut a small tree and took it home to his family. To recreate the effect of the stars, he placed candles on all its branches.

# THE CHRISTMAS TREE
## ACROSS THE WORLD

Early Christmas trees, harking back to pre-Christian times, had, in place of angels, figures of fairies – the good spirits – while horns and bells were placed on it to frighten off evil spirits.

In POLAND, Christmas trees were always decorated with angels, peacocks and other birds as well as many, many stars. In SWEDEN, trees are decorated with brightly painted wooden ornaments and straw figures of animals and children. In DENMARK, tiny Danish flags, along with mobiles of bells, stars, snowflakes and hearts are hung on Christmas trees. JAPANESE Christians prefer tiny fans and paper lanterns. LITHUANIANS cover their trees with straw bird cages, stars, and geometric shapes. The straw sends a wish for good crops in the coming year. CZECHOSLOVAKIAN trees display ornaments made from painted egg shells. In the UKRAINE every Christmas tree has a spider and web for good luck. Legend has it that a poor woman with nothing to put on her children's tree woke on Christmas morning to find the branches covered with spider webs turned to silver by the rising sun.

In BRITAIN, the custom of a decorated Christmas tree appears to have started in the early nineteenth century, when Albert, the Prince Consort to Queen Victoria, brought the tradition from his homeland of Saxe-Coburg, now part of Germany. The example set by royalty became a general fashion.

# THE CHRISTMAS STAR

In POLAND, they hold the Festival of the Star. Right after the Christmas Eve meal, the village priest acts as the 'Star Man' and tests the children's knowledge of religion. In ALASKA, boys and girls carry a star-shaped figure from house to house and sing carols in hopes of receiving treats. In HUNGARY a star-shaped pattern is carved in a half of an apple and is supposed to bring good luck.

# IN THE BLEAK MID-WINTER

CHRISTINA ROSSETTI

In the bleak mid-winter
Frosty wind made moan,
Earth stood hard as iron,
Water like a stone;
Snow had fallen, snow on snow
Snow on snow,
In the bleak mid-winter,
Long ago.

Our God, heav'n cannot hold Him
Nor earth sustain;
Heav'n and earth shall flee away
When He comes to reign;
In the bleak mid-winter
A stable place sufficed
The Lord God Almighty
Jesus Christ.

Enough for Him, whom Cherubim
Worship night and day,
A breastful of milk,
And a mangerful of hay;
Enough for Him, whom angels
Fall down before,
The ox and ass and camel
Which adore.

What can I give him,
Poor as I am?
If I were a shepherd
I would bring a lamb;
If I were a wise man
I would do my part;
Yet what I can I give Him
Give my heart.

# THE GLOW-WORM'S GIFT

At the time of the Nativity, legend tells us, the glow-worm did not possess the light which today is its distinguishing feature. A small, inconspicuous brown beetle, it went about its life unnoticed among the leaves and the grass. And would have remained so if one of them had not happened to be in a field by the stable at the time of Christ's birth. The little insect realized something very wonderful had taken place when she heard the angels singing and saw the shepherds stumbling through the fields in a hurry to see the infant Jesus. From the bigger insects she heard how, from all around, people and animals were flocking to the stable, and how the Wise Men were coming from the East, all bearing gifts to lay before the newborn King. She longed to join in the worship, even though she knew it would be a long and difficult journey across the field for a creature as small as herself. And she had no offering to take Him. But she so wanted to go, and then she remembered she had one prized possession – a hayseed. She could take that. But, she asked herself, what use would it be to the holy Baby, to the King of Heaven? It was all she had, though, and perhaps He would know this, and would not scorn her offering.

So she set off, pushing and dragging the hayseed, struggling through the thick forest of grass and weeds. After many exhausting days, she reached the stable, where she had an arduous climb up into the manger. But, at last, unseen by the crowd of worshippers, she reached the Christ Child and laid her minute gift next to him. No one else saw it, but the Baby did. He gurgled and stretched out His hand, and gently touched the tiny creature that had made such a laborious journey for Him. And as His finger fell softly upon her, her drab little body suddenly glowed with a shining light.

# A Christmas Tree

Charles Dickens

Encircled by the social thoughts of Christmas-time, still let the benignant figure of my childhood stand unchanged. In every cheerful image and suggestion the season brings, may the bright star that rested above the poor roof, be the star of all the Christian world!

# The Magi Visit the Christ Child

Then Herod, when he had privily called the wise men,
enquired of them diligently what time the star had appeared.

And he sent them to Bethlehem, and said, Go and search
diligently for the young child; and when ye have found him,
bring me word again, that I may come and worship him also.

When they had heard the king, they departed; and, lo, the
star which they saw in the east, went before them, till it
came and stood over where the young child was.

When they saw the star, they rejoiced with exceeding
great joy.

And when they were come into the house, they saw
the young child with Mary his mother, and fell down,
and worshipped him: and when they had opened their
treasures, they presented unto him gifts; gold, and
frankincense, and myrrh.

And being warned of God in a dream that they should not
return to Herod, they departed into their own country
another way.

MATTHEW 2: 7-12

# A Hymn on the Nativity of My Saviour

I sing the birth was born tonight,
The Author both of life and light;
The angels so did sound it,
And like the ravished shepherds said,
Who saw the light, and were afraid,
Yet searched, and true they found it.

BEN JONSON

# O HOLY NIGHT

O holy night!
The stars are brightly shining
It is the night of the dear Saviour's birth!
Long lay the world in sin and error pining,
Till he appear'd and the soul felt its worth.
A thrill of hope the weary world rejoices
For yonder breaks a new and glorious morn!
Fall on your knees
O hear the angel voices
O night divine
O night when Christ was born
O night divine
O night divine.
Led by the light of Faith serenely beaming,
With glowing hearts by His cradle we stand.
So led by light of a star sweetly gleaming,
Here come the wise men from Orient land.
The King of Kings lay thus in lowly manger,
In all our trials born to be our friend.
Truly He taught us to love one another.
His law is love and His gospel is peace.
Chains shall He break, for the slave is our brother
And in His name all oppression shall cease.
Sweet hymns of joy in grateful chorus raise we,
Let all within us praise His holy name.

# THE SWORD IN THE STONE

T. H. WHITE

It was Christmas night in the Castle of the Forest Sauvage, and all around the castle the snow lay as it ought to lie. It hung heavily on the battlements, like extremely thick icing on a very good cake, and in a few convenient places it modestly turned itself into the clearest icicles of the greatest possible length. It hung on the boughs of the forest trees in rounded lumps, even better than apple-blossom, and occasionally slid off the roofs of the village when it saw a chance of falling upon some amusing character and giving pleasure to all.

The boys made snowballs with it, but never put

stones in them to hurt each other, and the dogs, when they were taken out to scombre, bit and rolled in it, and looked surprised but delighted when they vanished into deeper drifts. There was skating on the moat, which roared all day with the gliding steel, while hot chestnuts and spiced mead were served on the bank to all and sundry. The owls hooted. The cooks put out all the crumbs they could for the small birds. The villagers brought out their red mufflers. Sir Ector's face shone redder even than these. And reddest of all shone the cottage fires all down the main street of an evening, while the winds howled outside and the old English wolves wandered about slavering in an appropriate manner, or sometimes peeping in at the keyholes with their blood-red eyes.

# SUSSEX CAROL

On Christmas night all Christians sing,
To hear the news the angels bring –
News of great joy, news of great mirth,
News of our merciful King's birth.

Then why should men on earth be so sad,
Since our Redeemer made us glad,
When from our sin he set us free,
All for to gain our liberty?

When sin departs before his grace,
Then life and health come in its place:
Angels and men with joy may sing,
All for to see the newborn King.

All out of darkness we have light,
Which made the angels sing this night:
'Glory to God and peace to men,
Now and for evermore. Amen.'

# CHRIST'S NATIVITY

HENRY VAUGHAN

Awake, glad heart! Get up and sing,
It is the birthday of thy King,
Awake! Awake!
The sun doth shake
Light from his locks, and all the way
Breathing perfumes, doth spice the day.

# MISTLETOE

Mistletoe was thought to be sacred by ancient Europeans. Druid priests employed it in their sacrifices to the gods, while Celtic people believed it to possess miraculous healing powers: in fact, in the Celtic language 'mistletoe' means 'all-heal'. It not only cured diseases, but could also render poisons harmless, make humans and animals prolific, keep one safe from witchcraft, protect the house from ghosts and even make them speak. With all of this, it was thought to bring good luck to anyone privileged to have it.

In a Norse myth, the story goes that mistletoe was the sacred plant of Frigga, goddess of love and the mother of Balder, the god of the summer sun. Balder had a dream of death, which greatly alarmed his mother, for should he die, all life on earth would end. In an attempt to keep this from happening, Frigga went at once to air, fire, water, earth, and every animal and plant, seeking a promise that no harm would come to her son. Balder now could not be hurt by anything on earth or under the earth. But Balder had one enemy, Loki, the god of evil, and he knew of one plant that Frigga had overlooked in her quest to keep her son safe. It grew neither on the earth nor under the earth, but on apple and oak trees. The lowly mistletoe. So Loki made an arrow tip of the mistletoe, which he gave to the blind god of winter, Hoder, who shot it, striking Balder dead. The sky paled and all things in earth and heaven wept for the sun god. For three days each element tried to bring Balder back to life. From the underworld was brought the message that if everybody wept for Balder he would be allowed to return to earth. And everywhere all living things wept, the mistletoe most of all, its tears becoming pearly white berries, while in her gratitude Frigga kissed everyone who passed beneath the tree on which it grew. The story ends with a decree that who should ever stand under the humble mistletoe, no harm should befall them, only a kiss, a token of love.

Later, the eighteenth-century English credited mistletoe not with miraculous healing powers, but with a certain magical appeal called a kissing ball. At Christmas time a young lady standing under a ball of mistletoe, brightly trimmed with evergreens, ribbons, and ornaments, cannot refuse to be kissed. Such a kiss could mean deep romance or lasting friendship and goodwill. If the girl remained unkissed, she might not expect to marry the following year. Whether we believe it or not, it always makes for fun and frolics at Christmas celebrations.

# IVY

Ivy has been a symbol of eternal life in the pagan world and then came to represent new promise and eternal life in the Christian world.

# ROSEMARY

Rosemary is yet another Christmas green. Though now it is used mainly to flavour foods, during the Middle Ages it was spread on the floor at Christmas. As people walked on it, the fragrant smell rose up to fill the house. The story goes that Mary laid the garments of the Christ Child over the shrub, which gave it its aroma. It is also said that rosemary is extremely offensive to evil spirits, thus being well suited to the advent of their Conqueror. In addition, the name rosemary associated as it is with the Virgin Mary's name, makes it all the more fitting for the Christmas season.

# THE CHRISTMAS ROSE

The Christmas rose, sometimes called the snow or winter rose, is in fact not a rose at all, but a hellebore. It blooms in the depths of winter in the mountains of Central Europe, but may be found in many English gardens. Legend links it with the birth of Christ and a little shepherdess named Madelon.

As Madelon tended her sheep one cold and wintry night, wise men and other shepherds passed by the snow-covered field where she was with their gifts for the Christ Child. The wise men carried the rich gifts of gold, myrrh and frankincense, and the shepherds, fruits, honey and doves. Poor Madelon began to weep for she had nothing at all for the newborn King. An angel, seeing her tears, flew down and before her astonished eyes brushed away the snow revealing a most beautiful white flower tipped with pink – the Christmas rose.

# Unto Us is Born a Son

Unto us is born a son!
King of all creation.
Came he to a world forlorn,
The Lord of ev'ry nation.
Cradled in a stall was he,
With sleepy cows and asses;
But the very beasts could see
That he all men surpasses.
Herod then with fear was filled:
'A prince,' he said, 'in Jewry!'

All the little boys he killed
At Bethlem in his fury.
Now may Mary's son, who came
So long ago to love us,
Lead us all with hearts aflame
Unto the joys above us.
Omega and Alpha he!
Let the organ thunder,
While the choir with peals of glee
Doth rend the air asunder.

# A Christmas Carol

GEORGE WITHER

So now is come our joyful feast,
Let every man be jolly;
Each room with ivy leaves is dressed,
And every post with holly.
Though some churls at our mirth repine,
Round your foreheads garlands twine,
Drown sorrow in a cup of wine,
And let us all be merry.

# DECK THE HALL

Deck the hall with boughs of holly, Fa la la la la la la la la!
'Tis the season to be jolly, Fa la la la la la la la la!
Don we now our gay apparel, Fa la la la la la la la la!
Troll the ancient Yuletide carol, Fa la la la la la la la la!

See the blazing yule before us, Fa la la la la la la la la!
Strike the harp and join the chorus, Fa la la la la la la la la!
Follow me in merry measure, Fa la la la la la la la la!
While I tell of Yuletide treasure, Fa la la la la la la la la!

Fast away the old year passes, Fa la la la la la la la la!
Hail the new, ye lads and lasses, Fa la la la la la la la la!
Sing we joyous all together! Fa la la la la la la la la!
Heedless of the wind and weather, Fa la la la la la la la la!

# HOLLY

Druids believed that holly, with its shiny leaves and red berries, stayed green to keep the earth beautiful when the sacred oak lost it leaves. They wore sprigs of holly in their hair when they went into the forest to watch their priests cut the sacred mistletoe.

Holly was the sacred plant of Saturn and was used at the Roman Saturnalia festival to honour him. Romans gave one another holly wreaths and carried them about, decorating images of Saturn with it. Centuries later, in December, while other Romans continued their pagan worship,

Christians celebrated the birth of Jesus. To avoid persecution, they decked their homes with Saturnalia holly. As Christian numbers increased and their customs prevailed, holly lost its pagan association and became a symbol of Christmas.

The plant has come to stand for peace and joy, people are said to settle arguments under a holly tree. It is believed to frighten off witches and protect the home from thunder and lightning. In GERMANY, a piece that has been used in church decorations is regarded as a charm against lightning. In western ENGLAND it is said that sprigs of holly around a young girl's bed on Christmas Eve are supposed to keep away mischievous goblins. And some British farmers put sprigs of holly on their beehives. On the first Christmas, they believed, the bees hummed in honour of the Christ Child. The English also mention the 'he holly and the she holly' as being the determining factor in who will rule the household in the following year, the 'she holly' having smooth leaves and the 'he holly' having prickly ones.

Other beliefs included putting a sprig of holly on the bedpost to bring sweet dreams and making a tonic from holly to cure a cough. Enough reasons for decking the hall with boughs of holly.

# ON THE MORNING OF CHRIST'S NATIVITY

JOHN MILTON

This is the month, and this the happy morn
Wherein the Son of Heav'n's eternal King,
Of wedded Maid, and Virgin Mother born,
Our great redemption from above did bring;
For so the holy sages once did sing,
That he our deadly forfeit should release,
And with his Father work us a perpetual peace.

# THE POINSETTIA

The legend of the poinsettia comes from Mexico. It tells of a girl named Maria and her little brother Pablo. They were very poor but always looked forward to the Christmas festival. Each year a large manger scene was set up in the village church, and the days before Christmas were filled with parades and parties. The two children loved Christmas but were always saddened because they had no money to buy presents. They especially wished that they could give something to the church for the Baby Jesus. But they had nothing.

One Christmas Eve, Maria and Pablo set out for church to attend the service. On their way they picked some weeds growing along the roadside and decided to take them as their gift to the Baby Jesus in the manger scene. Of course, other children teased them when they arrived with their gift, but they said nothing, for they knew they had given what they could. Maria and Pablo began placing the green plants around the manger and, miraculously, the green top leaves turned into bright red petals, and soon the manger was surrounded by beautiful star-like flowers and so we see them today.

# FATHER CHRISTMAS

Santa Claus, legendary bringer of gifts at Christmas, is generally depicted as a fat, jolly man with a white beard, dressed in a red suit trimmed with white, and driving a sleigh full of toys, drawn through the air by eight reindeer. Santa (also called Saint Nicholas and Saint Nick) is said to visit on Christmas Eve, entering houses through the chimney to leave presents under the Christmas tree and in the stockings of all good children. Although this familiar image of Santa Claus is a North American invention of the nineteenth century, it has ancient European roots and continues to influence the celebration of Christmas throughout the world.

The historical Saint Nicholas – Sankt Nikolaus in Germany and Sanct Herr Nicholaas or

Sinter Klaas in Holland – was venerated in early Christian legend for saving storm-tossed sailors, defending young children, and giving generous gifts to the poor. Although many of the stories about Saint Nicholas are of doubtful authenticity (for example, he is said to have delivered a bag of gold to a poor family by tossing it through a window), his legend spread throughout Europe, emphasizing his role as a traditional bringer of gifts. The Christian figure of Saint Nicholas replaced or incorporated various pagan gift-giving figures such as the Roman Befana and the Germanic Berchta and Knecht Ruprecht. In some countries Nicholas was said to ride through the sky on a horse. He was depicted wearing a bishop's robes and was said to be accompanied at times by Black Peter, an elf whose job was to whip any naughty children.